Lazarus Dot

A short story

A Felix Hoenniker Medical Murder Mystery

By Marc Arginteanu

Chapter One
Echoes of Addie

I tried not to think about the time: around 2AM.

I squeezed the bun (so soft).

I tried not to think about what and who was waiting for me at home: nothing and no one.

I watched a glistening teardrop of fat seep from the beef, drip onto a French fry, slither (so slow) along the golden shaft, plop onto the plate and congeal in an opaque puddle.

Josephine appeared at my side. "Can I bring you anything else, Doctor H?"

"I'm good," I answered, even though I wasn't. I didn't let Josephine's hard eyes loose until they melted a little and the crease around her mouth softened. I was the diner's lone patron. I felt like that guy in the Edward Hopper painting; you know the one.

Josephine splashed some coffee into my mug and drifted away.

If I were ever sentenced to death row (for my multitudinous sins) and awaiting the hangman, and if they granted my final request, they would shackle me like a beast and toss me in the county van. They would wedge me in this very same booth at the Golden Dove. And I would sit (in an orange jumpsuit) on this pleather bench at this stained Formica table one last time and...

My cell phone rang. *The Emergency Room*. A sigh escaped my lips, as if I'd been granted a last-minute reprieve. I said, "Doctor Hoenniker here."

"Felix," the ER doc said, breathlessly. "We need you as fast as your little wings can fly. I've got an eighteen-year-old girl in the trauma bay. But it doesn't look like a trauma. Quite honestly, I'm not sure what the heck is going on."

"Take a deep breath, Jim," I said. "What's the girl's name?"

He told me her name: Penelope Trojopoulos. I connected to the hospital and downloaded her scan on my cell phone. My mouth desiccated like desert dust. "Just eighteen years old you say?" That cheeseburger, so juicy on the way down, dried up and hardened into gravel in my gullet. "What's her exam like?"

"Her right pupil is blown."

"Fuck." My heart thumped against my ribs. "Intubate, hyperventilate and hang a bag of mannitol."

"This is not my first rodeo, Felix. Now get your skinny butt over here. Don't stop for any red lights."

"In this part of town?" I glanced through the plate glass at the bleak neighborhood. "I never do." Only a few windows were lit and those glared like menacing yellow eyes. "I barely tap the brakes."

I threw a Benjamin on the table. I nodded goodbye to Josephine. She didn't spare me a glance. She was in her own world: topping off the salt and pepper shakers: humming Bonnie Tyler's, *Holding Out for a Hero*.

I fired up the Maserati and flipped the top down. The night air would do me good… *The girl in the ER, Penelope, had one pupil blown, her brain was herniating: Swelling like a sopping wet sponge and shifting in her head: Arteries kinking like garden hoses, slowing the flow of blood to a trickle. Neurons flickering weakly, starving for oxygen…* I roared down the winding Staten Island streets. Tenements rose on my right and left like grimy canyon walls... *The mannitol will dry out her brain a little…* My wheel's kicked up grit. I took a turn too fast and my tires squealed... *The breathing tube and forced hyperventilation will help her brain too, decreasing the swelling, buying me some more time. Buying Penelope a few more precious moments…* I slammed on the brakes outside the ER and leapt out, leaving the Maserati double parked. *Time is brain.*

Jim met me at the door. Though straddling the hump of a double shift, his long white coat was crisp and his hair was perfect. "It's bedlam tonight, Felix," he said. Nurses ran past like chickens whose heads had been sawn off. Stretchers, filled with groaning patients, jam-packed every nook and cranny and spilled out into the hallways.

"You're one of the few specialists whose promptness never disappoints," he said. He grimaced at my rumpled suit and the dollop of ketchup, which had dripped on my shirt. "Your wardrobe's another story, though."

The truth was, I hadn't been home since Wednesday and I looked it.

We walked past trauma bay number five. The air was pierced by high pitched wail. "Not for you, Felix," Jim said. Through an opening in the curtains, I spied the weeping behemoth: two hundred and fifty pounds and covered head to toe with tattoos. "Gunshot to the belly." He grabbed the arm of a passing nurse. "A hundred mics of fentanyl for the big fellow in five. Stat!"

She nodded.

"That screaming." Jim made a show of cramming his fingers in his ears. "Like nails on the blackboard. Why is it that every tiny scratch turns humongous gangbangers into whimpering little girly-men?"

"Where's Penelope?" I asked.

"You can't even manage a smile tonight, Felix?" Jim's eyes filled with the emotion I despised to my core… pity.

I gritted my teeth and almost said something I'd regret.

"If we can't make each other laugh, Felix, we'll drown in a tub of tears."

My jaw relaxed.

"I was only half joking about your fashion sense, though." Jim said.

Jim yanked the curtain back on trauma bay number three and there she was. When I laid eyes on her my heart ached. Even with that plastic tube jutting out of her mouth, there was no denying she was a stunner. The elegant curve of her neck would put Botticelli's Venus to shame. Her long, silky hair splayed across the pillow like a schoolboy's fantasy.

I jiggled the breathing tube. She didn't gag or cough or grimace. I asked Jim, "When was the last time she got any sedation?"

"None given."

"Fuck." I pulled back her eyelids and shone my cell phone flashlight through the windows to her soul. As Jim had told me over the phone, the right pupil was fixed and dilated. The left one, though, still reacted briskly.

"Do you think she's too far gone?" Jim asked. His face had grown weary.

"Only one pupil is blown," I said, then added, in an almost (but not quite) confident tone, "Young brains are resilient."

Jim's face flashed hope. But a deluge of doubt inundated his visage, washing the sparkle away, leaving his features stony.

"She's got a fighting chance," I added, as if to convince myself.

Jim's shoulders tensed, a soldier preparing for incoming ordnance.

"I'll have a better idea of her prognosis after I pop in a ventric."

"What can I do to help, Felix?"

"You're plenty busy tending to the rest of this zoo. Just send over a nurse to give me a hand."

Jim nodded and turned to leave. Hector barged through the curtain and collided with him. "Sorry, hoss," Hector said. Jim shook his head in disgust and stomped away. Hector turned his eager eye towards me. "Did I hear you say you need a hand, chief?"

Of all the neurosurgical residents, I sighed. *It had to be Hector.*

"What do we got here, chief?" Hector asked.

"Why don't you pull up the scan and you can tell me."

Hector typed in the girl's name, Penelope Trojopoulos. He spelled it wrong twice. But the third time was a charm; her CAT scan appeared on the monitor. I hoped he'd get the diagnosis wrong. "Whoa!" His eyes widened. "Massive hydrocephalus. Look at the size of those ventricles."

Damn, I thought. He'd gotten it right: Water on the brain. I couldn't banish him to the on-call room to study the textbook.

"And what do you think we should do about it?"

"We've got to relieve the pressure," Hector answered. He's confident. I'll give him that. "Pass a ventricular catheter through the right frontal lobe."

Double damn, I thought. *Right again.* Now I had no choice but to let him perform the procedure, popping in the ventric. "OK, Hector. You talk the talk. Let's see if you walk the walk."

"Yessss!" He said and pumped his fist.

The first storm cloud to appear on the Hector horizon was his ham-fisted shaving. When inserting a ventricular catheter, you barely need to expose a postage stamp of bare scalp. Especially in a pretty young girl. "Come on, Hector!" I chided. "Her family's already going to be scared shitless. They don't need to see her with a fucking Uncle Fester head."

"Doctor Silvers always shaves this much."

"I don't give a damn what Mike does. When you're working on my patient, you do it my way."

"Sure, chief, sure. Do you like the cut vertical or horizontal?"

"Horizontal. That way if we need to extend…" I continued the monologue as Hector made the incision, a firm, precise cut. I thought, *At least he knows how to handle a knife.* And I liked how his hands moved as he controlled the scalp bleeders. *No wasted motion.*

Then came the time for drilling through the skull. It's one thing to do it yourself. It's quite another to stand by, helplessly observing a resident's on the job training. I fiddled with the overhead lights until they spotlighted Hector's gore-spattered gloves.

He burred through the rock-hard outer layer without a hitch. He crowed, "I'm really getting the hang of this."

My heart skipped a few beats when the drill started wobbling in his hand. "You've got to control the drill, Hector." The wobbling worsened. My heart leapt to my throat. I wanted to grab the drill from him. "Hold onto it like it's your cock, damn it."

"Sure, chief, sure." The wobbling stopped. "It's just that, well, it feels like the bone suddenly got a lot softer."

"That's fine. That's fine. You must've gotten into the middle layer." I sighed in relief. The middle layer is a relatively safe place for a drill to be. "It's typically spongy. As you get to the inner table, you'll feel it get hard again."

"Yeah," he said.

"Yeah, what?"

"The bone's hard again. Just like you said, chief. This drill's a real beut. Smooth. You know, one time—"

"Just concentrate on what you're doing, Hector," I said. "You've got to sort of push and pull at the same time otherwise you'll plunge into her brain."

"We've got a little problem here, chief." Hector held the drill aloft.

"Where's the bit?" I asked.

The drill bit had broken off in her skull. It was sticking out of her scalp like an antenna. Hector had just turned a fifteen-minute bedside procedure, which could be done in the trauma bay, into a clusterfuck. We had no choice but to rush her up to the Operating Room and try to un-fuck her.

Time is brain, I thought. And Penelope's hourglass was quickly running out of sand.

Like Charon, the ferryman, I'd accompanied Penelope from trauma bay number three to operating room number three and finally deposited her inert form in intensive care unit bed number three. Now, I was standing before her ICU room for the third day in a row.

I closed my eyes for a moment, gathering the strength to cross the threshold. The steady rhythm, *beep, beep, beep*, announced Penelope's heart's dogged persistence. The curtain spread apart and my own heart sang. Through the opening strode a slender young woman. She moved with the grace of a swan. The glowing lights surrounded her like a halo. Her pretty face radiated vigor.

Of course, it wasn't Penelope. If you were expecting a miracle cure, let me tell you right now, you're reading the wrong story. It was Penelope's nurse.

"Any improvement?" I asked.

She shook her head, no.

Hector's voice boomed from the other side of the ICU. "Pee-eww!" He said. "There's nothing like the smell of melena in the morning, am I right?" The old man in ICU bed number one had gastrointestinal bleeding, which had created a pervasive stench as it collected in his diaper. "Grab me a cup of coffee, would you, babe," he called to a nurse. "Holy cow! Cookies. Just what the doctor ordered. Who made these?"

I felt his hand on my shoulder.

"Hey, chief," Hector said, his mouth full. "You've got to try one of these." His lips were dusted with powdered sugar. He proffered a kourabiedes, which Penelope's mother had baked and just delivered to the nurse's station. She'd baked moustokouloura the day before. And the day before that, melomakarona. "They're out of this world."

I grabbed the cookie, crushed it in my fist and hurled the pulverized crumbs into the trash.

Hector blushed. He drew close to me. So close, in fact, I felt his hot breath on my cheek. He said, in a whisper, "I know I fucked up, chief. I fucked up, big time." At least he'd brushed his teeth that morning. "But I can only say I'm sorry so many times."

I sighed and wiped my sugary hands on my long white coat. There was no way around it. The next generation needed training and the road to competence was littered with fuck ups. Didn't I know that all too well? Besides, at the end of the day, it wasn't Hector's fault: the buck stopped with me. My shoulders slumped under the weight of the charnel house I lugged on my back. And now Penelope Trojopoulos joined the list of those injured and dead, who'd haunt me forever.

Hector, sensing the storm had passed, continued in a normal voice. "You can only do your best to help. And it's not like I caused her hydrocephalus. It wasn't like I sold her the drugs or forced her to—"

"Drugs?" I asked. Was there a deadly designer drug percolating through the streets of Staten Island? My first thought was, *Addie*. "Did you say, 'Drugs'?"

Hector nodded and a cookie crumb tumbled from his three-day stubble. "The EMT said our girl here was found down in the bathroom of that hot new club at the end of Victory Boulevard. You know the one? They got a rad DJ. He blasts EDM until the crack of dawn. And the drugs are tossed around like gumdrops. Not that anyone is forcing anyone else to partake. It's like I always say, 'play stupid games, win stupid prizes'."

It couldn't be Addie, I thought. *She promised*. I asked Hector, "And you're certain it's drugs?"

"Sure, I'm sure, chief. Her tox screen came back positive."

Addie had disappeared after that wild night at Kurtz's. She said she was leaving New York forever. Heading for the west coast. She swore she'd never design another drug, let alone cook up another lethal batch. Her pretty eyes were so earnest, I couldn't help but believe her. But they were also desperate, as if she were running from the devil.

"It's weird, though," Hector said. "I've never heard of any kind of drug that could cause what we saw on that CAT scan. And another thing, the lab couldn't identify it. Not exactly anyway. You look a little pale, chief."

"Addie," I mumbled.

"You're right, chief. It doesn't add up. Hey, you want to sit down?" Hector yelled to the ward secretary. "Grab Doctor Hoenniker a cup of coffee, would you, sweetheart." He turned back to me, "The organ transplant team wants to set up a meeting with her family and…"

Hector's prattle faded away, as did the glare of fluorescent lights and smells of melena and Clorox. I drifted somewhere faraway, slowly drowning in the honeysuckle of Addie's perfume.

Chapter Two

Saint Nicholas

It was the kind of day that would have been perfect for a wedding: light breeze, blue skies, cheerfully chirping birds. The sunlight coated everything and everyone like a layer of varnish. I'd arrived early and parked half a mile down the road. I walked slowly, past humble but well-kept homes. As I drew nearer, the gilded cross, mounted atop the church, beckoned me like a sweet song.

Like a stream feeding into a river, I trickled into the ever-expanding throng gathered before the threshold. Pressed on all sides by the congregation, I no longer found the sunlight pleasant, rather an enemy, against whose glare I squinted. Beads of sweat formed and fattened and dripped down my forehead. Later on, the full-page obituary in the *Staten Island Advance* would report an attendance of more than a thousand souls at Penelope Trojopoulos' funeral. It sure felt that way.

Three ponderous oaken doors swung open. The dam had broken. I was swept along by the crowd, which bucked gravity and flowed up the stone stairs and swirled into Saint Nicholas. *When was the last time I even stepped foot inside a church?* I wondered. My eyes drifted upwards and across the soffited dome. Of course, Jesus took center stage in the fresco. But it wasn't just Him judging me. He was surrounded by angels and saints, each of whom seemed to find me wanting.

Waiting for the service to begin, the crowd milled about, conversing in hushed tones. I did my best to blend in. But my long, lean frame and ever-searching eyes made being unobtrusive all but impossible. *Is it too late for me to escape?* I wondered. I tried to slip away, but steely fingers gripped my arm.

"Doctor H!" Penelope's father pressed into my side. "I can't believe you'd show up here."

"Well, Mister Trojopoulos, I just wanted to—"

"Metera," he called. His hand was inhumanly powerful, squeezing my flesh like a python's coils. "Metera." He dragged me towards the casket. The crowd split before us like the Red Sea. He stopped at the first row of pews. "Metera." An old, bent woman dressed in black, rocked like a boat. "Look who showed up."

Penelope's grandmother turned her puffy red eyes towards me.

Penelope's father spoke to her, in Greek.

The old lady spoke to me, in Greek.

I don't understand a word of Greek. A stupid joke bubbled up in my brain, *It's all Greek to me.* Perversely, laughter bubbled up behind my lips. I bit my tongue until a tear came to my eye.

The grandmother broke down, sobbing heavily. She blew her nose in a lacy handkerchief and then shook an arthritic finger at me. She continued speaking, her voice grew louder and louder.

The crowd encircling us grew quieter and quieter. Heads nodded in agreement. I guess they all spoke Greek, too. A thousand eyes locked upon me.

I gulped.

The old woman threw her arms around me. She squeezed my torso, tight as a noose. She was nearly as strong as her son. It was hard to draw a breath. She buried her head in my rumpled shirt and heaved with sobs.

"She said…" Mister Trojopoulos choked back a sob. "She said… she wants you to know…" The dam broke and twin rivers of tears coursed down his ashen cheeks.

Penelope's mother, a handsome middle-aged woman, wrapped an arm around her husband's shoulders. "My mother-in-law thanks you for all you did for Penelope. She thanks you for fighting so hard to save her. She… we can never repay you. She prays Jesus will keep blessing your hands and guiding your heart." She cleared her throat. "Some things are beyond the power of human comprehension." She shook her head. "She thanks you for doing your best. We all do."

I'd certainly done my job, that was true. The next generation of neurosurgeons had to learn their trade somehow. After all, one day I'd be dust and Hector (or someone like him) would need to fill my shoes. Yes, I'd done my job. But had I done my best? I gazed at the painted figures above me. I shuddered at the judgment that awaited.

An awed silence settled over the church. The only sound, as the Reverend Father floated to the pulpit, was his gold-trimmed gown, which flapped like a dove's wings. The service began and the priest's mellifluous voice anointed our aching souls. His grand gesticulations were reflected upon the lacquered surface of Penelope's casket, which lay between the priest and his flock. On account of Hector's botched scalp shave, the coffin was closed.

Between the priest's words, a barely audible sound took form. The kind you have to strain to hear. It grew insistent. *Tap, tap, tap,* like raindrops on Saint Nicholas' domed roof. *That's strange,* I thought. *There wasn't a cloud in the sky.* The sound tapered off for a little while and then grew louder. This time, it wasn't like rain. It wasn't like thunder, either. It was like… like the percussion of slender sticks on a drum. Intermittent at first, it became more steady. It grew deeper and deeper in tone, until it thumped like a whale's heart and echoed through the church.

Murmurs from the crowd: "Hey, you hear that?" "What gives?"

The Reverend Father stopped speaking and cocked his head. For a moment, the church became as silent as midnight snow. Then came the noise: *Thump. Thump. Thump.*

"It can't be," someone behind me gasped. "That sound… it's coming from the coffin."

Thump. Thump. Thump.

More gasps.

The casket began to shake. Its smooth cedar surface was littered with rose petals, which shimmied off the lid and fluttered to the ground like butterfly wings.

Screams and gasps.

The head panel burst open. The interior of the coffin was exposed and we all gawked: white satin lining: pure as a wedding gown. Penelope sat bolt upright. The cross (which had been placed on her bosom) and the icon (which had been on her forehead) flew across the room. Deafening shouts and screams filled my ears.

The mortician was a master of his craft. Despite the missing patch of hair, Penelope glowed with holy beauty. She made time stand still as only a lovely young girl can. Her soft cheeks turned upwards in adoration of the soffited dome. Her gently closed eyes mocked death as a distant dream. The throng fell silent and stared in awe. We weren't certain what we were witnessing but it sure seemed like a miracle.

Penelope's mouth dropped opened in a silent scream. Within the space of a few heartbeats, the angelic makeup (so artistically painted by the embalmer) melted from her face and neck, as if she were a nightmarish popsicle. Her skin sloughed, flowing into her lacy white gown. Her silky hair clumped and slid down her back like mud. Her muscle and sinew liquefied. Her eyeballs rolled into her skull and her bones involuted.

The faithful souls of Saint Nicholas descended into barbarity. Pews were flipped as most rushed headlong towards the doors. The weakest and slowest were shoved mercilessly. Some dropped to their knees and prayed, only to be trampled. The priest, up on the pulpit, tore his gown and wept. Penelope's old, bent grandmother trembled like a leaf. I joined hands with her son. We wrapped our arms around her, shielding her from the heaving mob.

"Oh, Addie," I cried. "Why? Why didn't you leave well enough alone?" My shouts were swallowed by the tumult.

Chapter Three
Lazarus Dot

I couldn't help but laugh when I read the front-page headline: The Final Flail in the Coffin. Of course, I felt like a Major League asshole for laughing. After all, yet another person lay dead and his teenage body desecrated. Then, I remembered Jim's words, *If we can't make each other laugh, we'll drown in an tub of tears*. I still felt like an asshole, but maybe Minor League.

I tossed the tabloid onto the wrought iron table. A veritable parade of zombies had been splashed across the pages of the *New York Post* during the preceding week. Besides Penelope, six others had overdosed on the horrific designer drug, dubbed the Lazarus Dot. The first part of the moniker was self-explanatory: each victim remained tethered to this world for a fleeting resurrection. They'd called the drug a Dot because, when cops had got hold of a batch, they discovered it was meant to be licked from the back of Keith-Haring-graffiti-covered stamps. They also said it smelled like Flintstone's vitamins. The victims, of course, had all been young people. Cut down in the prime of life; the oldest had been thirty-two. One of the poor bastards flopped off the autopsy table then sizzled, popped and melted into a grisly puddle, which sloshed around the coroner's shoes.

I flipped a bit of Wonder Bread to a pigeon (he was ambling across my terrace). The fat bird pecked the toasted crust into beak-sized crumbs. I was glad not to be eating alone. I polished off my brunch, savoring each bite of bacon (perfectly crispy). The bird and I watched a cloud bank steamroll across New York Harbor and blanket the mighty Verrazano Bridge's pylon towers.

"It must have been Addie," I announced. "Who else could pull something like this off?"

The pigeon answered, "Coo. Coo. Coo."

"Easy for you to say, my feathered friend." The falling drizzle coated my face, but I didn't mind. Rainy days were made for thinking and I really needed to think.

The pigeon eyed me. He clearly had something on his mind too.

"Here you go," I flung my final crust, hoping to coax some wisdom.

"Coo. Coo. Coo."

"Yeah," I said. "I know she promised. I want to believe her. I really do… You think maybe somebody hijacked her lab or stole her cookbook?"

The bird hopped off the parapet and flapped into the mist.

Addie, I shook my head. The last time I'd seen her was that night in Kurtz's mansion. Our bodies were so tantalizingly close, but all she let me do was dance. And much to my shame, I'll never amount to much at the tango. Of course, I tried for more. But she pushed me away (none too gently). Sure, I get it. It's hard to get into the mood when you're surrounded by dead bodies. And, sure, her daughter D.D. might have barged in on us any minute. But at least she could've let me cop a feel… or plant a kiss (tender or rough, pick your poison) on her long, slender neck.

"Her neck," I said to the iron-gray sky. "That's it." At the intersection of Addie's shoulder, back and neck was that tattoo: arcane symbols and letters from a long-forgotten tongue cast in twisting, intertwining, concentric circles. Even thinking about her tattoo made me feel as if I would float into the ominous sky and drift away like a lost balloon.

"The tattoo." Yes, that's how I'd find Addie. I've only ever seen an emblem like that once before: engraved into the door of my favorite pub: Azazel's. I had to figure out where she got it.

I turned the corner and smiled and thought, *Holly always knows what I need.*

Usually what I needed from Holly involved a tumbler overflowing with Blanton's. But on that drizzly afternoon I had a specific question in mind: Where does someone go to get branded with an Azazel's tattoo? I mean, not every Tom, Dick or Harry has

15

the skills to lay down that kind of ink. I hoped Holly could give me a lead. Of course, I'd take the whiskey too.

My feet guided me towards Azazel's automatically, without any input from my brain. No surprise there. After all, it was a path I'd trod more times than I'd care to admit. How often? Let's put it this way: like Glen Campbell's *Rhinestone Cowboy*, I knew every crack in that dirty sidewalk.

But today, something seemed strange. "Nah," I told myself. "My eyes are just bleary from all this mist." After all, it wasn't just any old drizzle. Staten Island precipitation is chock full of acid and soot. It was more than rain in my eyes, though. The sidewalk really did seem more uneven than ever before, maybe even rocking a little, like a barge in the bay. The cracks seemed to have grown wider, too. The weeds poking through the chasms were nasty, clinging to my trouser legs like the tentacles of my sordid past. Even the fat cockroaches eyed me brazenly.

I arrived at my destination and swiveled towards the squat building which housed Azazel's. *What the hell is going on?* Instead of facing the familiar carved portal and orange brick façade, my eyes were struck by graffiti covered plywood boards. *When did this happen? I was just here on… Hmm, wait a minute… When was the last time?* I racked my brain but couldn't put a finger on it. *Yesterday? A week ago? Last month?*

A middle-aged woman leapt over a sidewalk abyss, as if there were trolls ensconced in the shadowy depths, clawing at the hem of her skirt.

I said, "Excuse me."

She bent her head and hurried by.

"Excuse me," I repeated, using my most authoritative doctor voice.

She turned tentatively towards me.

"Since when," I asked, "has Azazel's been closed?"

She crossed herself and scurried away.

Curiouser and curiouser, I thought. I leaned against an old station wagon. Like that of many of the cars parked along the curb, its paint bubbled like leprous skin (rust invaded its body, bit by bit). My eyes roamed up and down the block, across bleak doorways and concrete stoops. The row homes lining the street had been elegant when they were first built. That was long ago, though, when each housed a single family. At least three families, one family per floor, currently resided in each.

They've got to be stuffed with kids. Kids who would be pouring out any second to play stickball (or something) in the street. Kids who must have some answers about Azazel's.

Not a soul emerged.

The drizzle turned to rain and I cast about the vacant gutter for a plan C. There were two storefronts along the street. The cheery, brightly lit Dunkin' Donuts was out of the question. First of all, I wasn't hungry. And secondly, coffee is a poor substitute for bourbon.

I turned towards the other store. The sign, which hung over the door, announced: Vinny's Shoes. The paint had peeled so badly, it read Vinny's oes. Another sign, edges curled and yellow, taped to the inside of the plate glass, announced: Going Out of Business. Everything 50% Off. I said to myself, "Who doesn't love a bargain?"

A bell tinkled (the merry sound seemed out of place) as I pushed through the door. The store was empty, save a man with a bad toupee. His head was bent low and his eyes were myopically glued to the sports pages of the *Staten Island Advance*. He slumped, half hidden by an ancient cash register. You know the type: a clunky metal machine; when you punch a key, a bell dings and a price decal pops up in the window.

I milled about, feigning interest in the dusty shelves which were crammed with sneakers, shoes, moccasins... They'd never been in style long enough to be out of style.

The proprietor paid me no mind. He thumbed through the paper. From time to time, he scoffed and grumbled at the broadsheet pages, "Damned Mets," or "Damned Jets."

Finally, I asked, "Are you Vinny?"

He fixed me with a 'can't you read the sign' glare and said, "Vinny went out of business." He looked me up and down suspiciously. His furrowed brows hung low over brooding eyes. He finally shook his head and turned his attention to a front-page article in the lifestyle section: How Blood and Bone Fertilizer Helped Me Grow Award Winning Tomatoes.

"You wouldn't happen to know," I ventured, "what happened to the place across the street?"

"Just what I figured," he scoffed. "You ain't in here to buy no shoes."

I settled into a worn and wobbly chair and stretched out my skinny legs. "I'm size eleven."

Not-Vinny disappeared behind a curtain. He moved quickly for a guy with a big paunch. He reappeared with a pile of boxes, which looked much too large for shoes. He plopped himself onto a shoe-fitting stool.

I began, "About Azazel's—"

He flinched at the name, as if I'd pricked him with a thorn.

"What happened..." I watched closely as I finished the question. "... to Azazel's?"

This time he didn't flinch. "Let's see," he cocked his head. "It was just the other day. Yeah, I was sleeping like a log. Then, there was this ear-splitting crash. Loud enough to wake the dead. Early in the morning, it was. Yeah, as I remember, the sun ain't even up yet." He used a well-worn measuring device to confirm my foot size. "I live upstairs." There was an apartment above the store. "Some clown crashed his U-haul through the front wall and ransacked the damned place. I don't know what anyone would've taken from that shit-hole."

Shit-hole, I thought. *That's the pot calling the kettle black.*

He grabbed my calves, yanked off my loafers and tossed them over his shoulder. His iron grip rivalled Penelope's father's. He plopped my feet down (none too gently) between his own stout legs, upon the rubber tread of the slanted footrest.

"Did you call the cops?"

He snickered, "Yeah, right."

"Wow. So, Azazel's is gone. That's too bad," I sighed. "It was one of my favorite pubs. A real hidden gem."

His furrowed brows corrugated and his coal-black eyes stomped all over me.

"It's just, I'll miss the place." The way he looked at me put me on the defensive and my tone sounded it. "I mean," I cleared my throat and evened out my tone. "I was something of a regular."

"Regular?" He scoffed. "You're way too young to have been a regular."

"What does that mean?" No one had accused me of looking young since the stubble on my chin and the hair around my temples had started to go gray.

"That place shut down in the 80's."

"What?" My jaw dropped. "You mean the 1980's?"

"Duh," he said.

"Are you shitting me?"

His eyes said otherwise.

Curiouser and curiouser. I held an outstretched hand in front of my face. Steady as ever. I wasn't going through DTs, so this all couldn't be some strange hallucination.

"You looking for a manicure?" He dug around his shirt pocket (a short-sleeve button-down bowling shirt with a frayed collar) and retrieved a business card from behind a crumpled pack of Camels. "Tell them Vin—, uh, tell them Vito sent you. You'll get ten percent off."

"Do I look like the kind of guy who gets manicures?"

"What you look like is the kind of guy who could use a brand new pair of boots."

"Boots?"

"Is there an echo in here?"

"Look, Vito." I said. "I've never worn a pair of boots in my life and—"

"What do you do for a living?"

"I'm a doctor."

"Do I tell you how to cure people?" He scoffed. "I didn't think so… Now just pipe down and let me do my job."

Could I have imagined it all? Could I be mixing Azazel's up with some other dive bar? The beer sticky floor… The splintery stools… Sure, I've drunk myself blind in lots and lots of places like that.

Vito slid a pair of boots onto my feet. "Nah, alligator ain't for you." His toupee shifted sideways as he grunted and yanked the stubborn footwear from my feet.

What about the long bar, as smooth as black ice? That bar is unique for sure. But could I have imagined it? Well, I guess it wasn't out of the realm of possibility.

"Cowhide?" Vito slid another pair on. He sat back, put his beefy hands on his thighs and scowled. "Nah, it don't make enough of a statement."

"No," I said, which Vito perceived as my agreement with his sartorial judgment. "No," I repeated. "She's for real." I could no more have imagined Holly's alabaster skin than I could be imagining the beating of my own heart or its fluttering at the eternal melancholy in her pure blue eyes.

"Yep," Vito leaned back and nodded. "These here are the ones." He beamed like a proud papa.

"Not bad," I said.

"Not bad," he glowered and gesticulated. "Not bad." He scoffed. "These here are the best boots you'll ever wear."

"What are all the little bumps?"

"That's where the feathers were. Ain't nobody makes ostrich boots like Lucchese."

"Lucchese?" I shook my head. Leave it to a Staten Islander to push Italian cowboy boots. "Look, Vito. If I'm going to get boots… and I'm not fully committed yet… I'd for sure want them born and bred in Texas."

"Since 1883. Says so right on the box." He opened his mouth to regale me with the Lucchese brothers' odyssey from Sicily to San Antonio but deemed me unworthy of the tale. "Why don't you give them a whirl."

I strolled around the well-worn carpet.

"You look sharp, doc," he smirked.

He read it in my strut… he'd made the sale.

"They're alright. Not very comfortable, though."

"They'll mold to your feet as you walk. They'll become part of you."

"Well, how much?"

"Your lucky day, doc. They're on sale. Eight-hundred bucks."

"Cash price?"

"Seven."

I sat down with a huff and yanked at the Luccheses.

"Six."

I pulled out my wad and peeled off half a dozen Benjamins.

My cash disappeared, lickety-split, into his shirt pocket, behind the Camels. "Doc," he said. "About that place."

I looked at him quizzically.

"You know." Vito glanced around furtively and lowered his voice. "Azazel's." He shuddered. "I wouldn't go poking my nose where it don't belong if I was you."

If I knew then what I know now, I would've listened to him. On second thought, I probably would've ignored his advice anyway. You only live once, after all. Why not make it eventful? Anyway, those boots sure as hell came in handy.

Chapter Four
Saint Adalbert

The cobblestones, buffed and polished by the weight of centuries and the passage of countless travelers, shone like black satin. They were hell on my wheels, though. I cursed through chattering teeth as I bumped along through the meatpacking district.

"There's a spot!" I said to no one. I parked the Maserati in a tow away zone, slid the 'Doctor on Medical Call' placard onto the dashboard and burst into the noonday sun.

"Not another one!" I soliloquized to no one. "You can't swing a dead cat in this damned neighborhood without hitting an old warehouse being gussied up and repackaged as a hive of gazillion-dollar lofts." I passed by a bevy of trendy restaurants. "I've got to admit, though, gentrification isn't all bad." The perfume of exotic delicacies spilled onto the street and, bit by bit, cloaked the ever-present miasma of garbage and stale urine.

My destination was the lone constant in the ever-changing district: an ivy-covered, brick townhouse (the narrowest in all of Manhattan) wedged between two Frankensteinian monstrosities. I descended the worn alabaster stairs and pushed through the door of the Scrivener's Club.

Rattling, like the shaking of a dozen snakes' tails, echoed through the subterranean twilight. I heard a shout of, "Felix," and waded through a cloud of cigar smoke towards the sound of my name. Grim faced men squared off across a dozen tables. Rolled dice clattered noisily over wooden backgammon boards. When the carved bones came to rest, their black dotted faces directed the movement of hand-carved checkers and, ultimately, determined the fate of mountains of cash.

I found Bartleby at his usual table, way in the back. "Well?"

"I couldn't find Addie." He threw his hands up. "She's… unfindable."

"You could have saved me the commute." I pushed my chair back and stood up. "The Verrazzano was bumper to bumper. You know I don't particularly care for—"

"Relax. Drinks are on me."

I sat back down.

"Hey, what is it with you and the city anyway?" Bartleby asked. "I guess all the freaks give you the heebie-jeebies?"

"Freaks are right up my alley. In fact, in my younger days… Well, I won't bore you with stories. What I don't like, especially in a neighborhood like this, is all the people who are pretending *not* to be freaks."

"Don't get all high and mighty on me, Felix. We're all pretenders. You, of all people, should know that." The way he looked at me made me glad it was too dark for him to have seen my brand-new ostrich skin cowboy boots. "It's more like… well, you've got to be careful who you pretend to be. If you do it hard enough and long enough, it comes true. Or nearly true, at least." He shuddered. "And don't I know that all too well."

The ancient, one-eyed attendant set down our drinks.

"Besides," Bartleby raised his chipped porcelain mug. "Where else can a guy get a cup of Joe like this? These here beans were plucked from a bush that grows on the side of a volcano." He sipped gingerly. "For real. You can almost taste the lava."

"I'm in the company of a real connoisseur," I said.

"I know what good is."

I raised my drink and we touched the brims. Though it was too dim to see my glass, I was certain it was filthy. I sipped. "Mmm." Rye. I sipped again. "Leathery." I set it down to ponder.

"Use your coaster," Bartleby scoffed. "I can't take you nowhere."

I sipped again. "Young and brash." I ventured, "Stellum?"

He nodded.

I tossed back the remainder. "Very nice." The grizzled attendant set down another. Dust from his eyepatch peppered the surface of my rye. "I still prefer the ambiance at Azazel's, though."

"Where?"

"You know, the place we met last time, when you helped me with the crooked cop thing."

"It ain't ringing no bells."

"You complimented the bar. It was a long wooden job. Completely seamless. Looked like it was hewn from the trunk of a mammoth tree. You said, 'This here's a thing of beauty'."

"No." He tugged and twisted the tips of his mustache. "I'd remember something like that. You know I love a good-grained wood. You sure it was me you were with?"

"Sure, I'm sure. Why, it was just last… last… hmm… when the hell was it?" I racked my brain but couldn't remember… Was it a week ago? Or maybe a month? I shook my head, "Ah, never mind."

"I do have something for you, by the way'" Bartleby said. He slid his chair next to mine and flipped open his laptop. "You didn't give me much to go by. Now, some guys, they don't like a challenge." By the excitement in his voice and the tremor in his fingers, I could tell the caffeine had kicked in. "I mean, D.D. Bundren at NYU. First of all, there ain't a single Bundren in the whole damned school… and D.D.?" he scoffed. "C'mon. Sure, it was a real challenge. But for a guy like me. Well." The glow of the screen lit up his kid-in-a-candy-store smile. "I searched Didi, Deedee, Deirdre and everything else under the sun. No Dice." He looked at me. "Want to take a guess at what D.D. is short for?" I opened my mouth. "You'll never get it. Not in a million years. Dewey Dell. Believe that? Who names their kid Dewey Dell. I'm betting it's not the mother. She's a scientist, you said. I bet the father saddled her with that gem of a name before he up and ditched them. In fact, that's about all he left his daughter, the family name. He's some freaky writer. Nothing anyone with any taste would read, though. So, of course, I found her, even though she dropped out of school last semester, then went and dropped off the grid… Dewy Dell Faulkner. She's renting out some space for cash. Dirt cheap, by the way. Over in Queens." He emailed me an address. "Elmhurst, to be exact."

I slapped six Benjamins down on the table. Three of the bills disappeared into Bartleby's vest pocket, right behind the antique watch on the gold chain. He slid the other three Benjamins back to me and said, "Six hundred was to find your girlfriend."

"Addie's not my girlfriend," I said. "Never was." I added, sadly, "Her choice, not mine."

"Whatever," Bartleby said. "Anyway, finding Addie's daughter might be a good lead… but it's only worth half, at most."

Parked on an Elmhurst side street, my Maserati would have stuck out like a sore thumb. So, I left the car in the meatpacking district, hopped on the R train and climbed out of the subway station. My mission was best left until the sun went down. I looked for a tavern to kill a few hours. "No open bars? What the hell kind of neighborhood is this?" For the second time in a month, I found myself sitting in a church. As a matter of fact, it was the second time in a decade, too.

There were differences between the churches, of course. Saint Adalbert, in whose pews I currently reposed, was Roman style. Saint Nicholas, where I'd all too recently witnessed the effects of the Lazarus Dot in all its in-glory, was the Greek variety. And, what's more, I was the only soul in Saint Adelbert. I'd been unmolested by any human presence as I silently gazed, hour after hour, at dust motes floating through the progressively slanting light. Saint Nicholas, on the other hand, on that mournful day, had been packed to the rafters.

The crucial thing remained the same, though. I'd felt that thing beaming from Saint Nicholas' soffited dome and now the same thing palpably streamed through Saint Adalbert's stained glass. I bet I'd feel the exact same thing if I were in a synagogue or mosque. It was that which called me to be better than I was. Now, if I could only find the strength to allow that thing into my heart.

After the sun disappeared, I descended the church steps and crossed 84th Street. There were few pedestrians and little traffic. All the neighborhood kids had been called in for dinner. Parked cars (old but well kept) lined the curb. Streetlights (glowing alien eyes on long metal necks) jutted from tar covered utility poles. I skulked past row houses (clad in unblemished aluminum siding and neatly painted window trim) and tried to shake the feeling that, despite my best intentions, I'd soon be injecting a dose of misery into the sedate neighborhood.

I double checked Bartleby's email. Yup, this was D.D.'s address. Hers was the final attached home in the row and a narrow alley separated it from a squat brick tenement. I hopped over the fence, and crept around, sticking like a mantis to the side of D.D.'s row home. In my experience, after someone's dropped off the grid, they don't answer when someone comes ringing at their doorbell.

I flipped over a trash can and struggled to set it down silently. The galvanized steel bottom was permeated with rust. It seemed like it would bear my weight, though. I climbed atop and peered into a darkened room. I tugged at the window, praying it would open without squeaking, and clambered in.

I tiptoed down the darkened hallway. A reedy voice spilled from the warm, brightly lit kitchen, "Fear not, young lady. If the shadow of a holy house caresses an abode, however humble, protection against the minions of the man downstairs, shall be conferred upon all those who dwell within."

"And it really says all that in there?" D.D.'s voice sounded uncharacteristically thick and slow.

"Upon my honor," her interlocutor intoned gravely. "Nevertheless, our numinous and hallowed order has not ensconced you thusly merely for the sake of your protection."

I stepped into the light and my jaw dropped. No wonder D.D.'s voice sounded so strange. Her lip was split wide open. Not only that, one of her eyes was purple and swollen shut.

A fat old man glared at her from across the Formica table. A brown felt fedora with a feather in the band was plastered to his head. A pearl-handled revolver was holstered to his chest. "No, I am charged with far more than the preservation of your corporeal form. Like myself, you're merely a player in a larger drama." He raised a fat finger in the air. "The latest incarnation of the scourge must be cleansed—"

"What the fuck did you do to her?" I shouted at the fat man. I turned to the girl. "Don't worry, D.D. I'm going to—"

D.D.'s uninjured eye locked upon me and grew wide with terror. "Did Mom send you?" She began to tremble.

"Your mother?" I shook my head. "Addie didn't send me… I'm looking for her."

"Wait." D.D's muscles relaxed. "What?" She cocked her head. "You're looking for her?"

"Egad!" The old man turned to me. His eyes were tinged with zealotry… or maybe insanity. "One of Preta's minions!"

"Preta?" I said, "What the hell's that?"

He jumped to his feet with the surprising grace of a fat man. "What manner of unholiness is this?" Keloids were scattered across his cheeks, as if his face had been splattered with dollops of pink bubble gum. "It defies all that is written." He glanced at an ancient tome, which lay open on the kitchen table.

D.D. stared at him, dubiously. "Are you sure he was sent by—"

He unholstered his revolver and leveled it at my chest. "Yet one cannot deny one's very senses." He sniffed the air and asked D.D. "Do you not detect the wafting aroma of licorice?"

"Um," she said, "not really."

"Beware! He's like to transmogrify into a jackal at any moment." The old man pulled the trigger. Deafening thunder filled the room.

I looked down at my chest. No holes.

I looked down at the old man. He lay sprawled across the floor. The kickback from the .357 magnum had sent him reeling.

There's nothing quite so exhilarating as being shot at without effect. I leapt forward and crunched the old man's right wrist under the heel of my brand new Lucchese. I wasn't going to let him get off another round. "One thing I've learned about shooting." I said, smugly. "You've really got to use two hands." I reached down and snatched his gun.

"Fly, young lady. Fly like the wind." The old man said. "You may yet survive to fight another day. I shall endeavor to keep the demonic cad at bay." He reared up. "Remember me fondly." His fedora, which had somehow remained in place so far, tumbled from his head, revealing scraggly strands of pale hair. "Sing of my exploits to your children." He sunk his teeth into my thigh.

"Owww!" I yelled. A few inches higher and I'd have been singing soprano. "What the fuck!"

D.D. flung open the refrigerator door and leapt inside.

"Let go." I yanked my leg but his teeth were clamped on tight. "You crazy old bastard." I thumped him on the head with the pearl handled butt of the revolver and that did the trick.

The fat man was stunned, but only for a moment. He shook his head like a wet dog and then he grabbed his hat. He spared me one last glance; his eyes were wild and his teeth stained with my blood. He turned tail and wriggled into the refrigerator like a greased pig. He yanked the door shut behind him.

I tugged at the handle. It didn't budge. I pulled harder, grunting and getting both hands and one foot in on the action. No dice. I rifled through the kitchen for something I could use to pry the refrigerator door open.

Then, that thing stopped me dead in my tracks. Time, which had been rushing by like a swollen river, froze solid. That thing that had caught my eye wouldn't let go.

I sat heavily on the chair (chrome tube and red pleather) and rested my elbows on the kitchen table. I stroked (so smooth) one of the ancient pages; crowded with line after line of black and red letters. No spaces separated the incomprehensible words from each other and no punctuation marks separated sentence from sentence. Black flourishes surrounded the text, as if to protect the writing from the illustrations, which lurked in the wide margins. Demons, serpents, wolves and vultures, embellished with blue and gold; hungry eyes boring into the arcane phrases; toothy mouths hanging agape; coiling muscles ready to spring.

Stiff parchment crackled in protest as I slowly leafed through yellow-edged pages. The margins were crowded with occult symbols, only a few of which were familiar: a golden ankh, a ruby red pentagram (a demon's face in the center and ancient symbols at each of its points), the all-seeing eye.

I flipped the vellum page again and began to shake like a leaf. There it was: The three intertwining rings, arcane symbols and ancient letters. The same as Addie's tattoo. The same as the emblem engraved on Azazel's door.

The book itself wasn't causing my trembling. It wasn't the Azazel's emblem either. Not directly at least. It was that thing. But it wasn't the same thing as before, in the church. It was quite the opposite. It was that which emboldened the shadowy part of myself and lured me towards darkness' embrace. Its sirens' song echoed louder and louder in my heart. How could I resist? My strength was stretched and stretched, like a rubber band about to snap.

I heard a wailing from the apartment upstairs: "Ayúdeme."

I rushed up the stairs, following the lamentations: "Ayúdeme."

A grade-school-aged girl with an angel's face and long dark hair swayed like a reed in the open doorway. Her head leaned backwards and her gaping mouth (framed by a combo of baby teeth and grown-up teeth, with some wide gaps thrown in) repeated the plaintive cry: "Ayúdeme."

A twenty-something man, with an appalling visage and the physique of a linebacker was sprawled on the couch, just beyond the little girl. I swept her aside and charged into a scene from the Texas Chainsaw Massacre. Based upon the blood splattered across the wall (and dripping from framed pictures of faraway landscapes) I could tell the fat man's errant bullet had blasted through one of the young man's arteries. Based upon the cherry-red pattern, painted on the snow-white cushions, I could tell the strength of the victim's heart was flagging: the young man was in the center of a rainbow with ever-decreasing arcs.

I turned to the little girl, "Tráigame la faja."

She nodded gravely; the fear had left her eyes. She whirled about. Her pink frilly Disney Princess dress swished as she disappeared into a back room.

His face was the color of chalk. His eyes were sunken and shut and he was too weak to moan. His ragged breathing sounded like the snores of a drunkard. I stepped closer to him and my boots splashed through an ever-widening ruddy puddle. I rearranged the cushions and positioned his head lower than his heart.

The little girl rushed back into the room holding a woman's girdle.

I scoffed and removed my own belt. I fashioned a tourniquet and strapped it on his thigh, directly above the bullet hole.

"Ah, cinturón," she said.

The sound of sirens reached my ears. I turned to leave.

"Quédate aquí," She begged. She'd wrapped her arms around my legs.

"I can't stay," I said. I didn't want to explain to the police why the gun, which had been used to blow a hole in her father, was stuffed in my pocket.

"Por favor." She gazed up at me with sloe eyes. I could tell she liked me. Little kids always like me. "Quédate."

"I've really got to go." I shook the little girl loose. Her embrace was surprisingly strong and cold, it felt icy through my trousers. "He'll be alright." The siren's cry grew ever louder. I couldn't bring myself to meet her gaze. "Papí, estará bien."

I felt her eyes boring into my back as I descended the stairs.

My pants slid over my narrow ass and fell halfway down my thighs. "That was my favorite belt," I groused. "The leather was like butter." I passed through D.D.'s kitchen on the way out. "The book's gone," I breathed a sigh of relief. At the same time, as I scanned the barren Formica table, aching hunger gnawed at my empty gut.

I gave the refrigerator a last try. It opened so easily I fell backwards. The bulb flickered like a winking demon. Shelves stuffed with garden variety groceries filled the space where D.D. and the fat man had passed moments earlier. "Curiouser and curiouser," I said.

The police banged on D.D.'s front door. I slipped out through the back door. I hopped fences and scurried through alleyways, hitching up my pants every few steps.

Chapter Five
Rick's of Secaucus

I limped out of the Emergency Room. A Kermit-the-frog-colored Volkswagen Camper Van was idling by the curb. It looked to be late '60s vintage. The rusty tailpipe blew little puffs of black smoke, which smelled like cancer. The passenger window was open. I leaned in and said, "Whoa! Where'd you score the groovy wheels?"

"I… I borrowed it," D.D. said. In the morning light, her face looked even more gruesome. The gash in her lip had cracked open and blood trickled around the crusty scab. "Alexei Fyodorovich… well, he won't be needing it." She smirked and then stretched-lip-pain flipped her smirk into a grimace. "Not for a while at least."

"Alex Whatever-ovich?" I asked. "Is that your bitey friend?"

She nodded. Her lone open eye shiftily wandered over the dashboard.

"D.D.," I said, all the humor in my voice melted away. "Was he the one who redecorated your face?"

"Alexei?" She erupted in a mirthless peal, which sounded like her mother. "Don't make me laugh." She blotted her bleeding lip with a Kleenex. "It hurts too much."

"Then tell me," I said, cranking the earnestness up a decibel. "Who the hell did this to you? I can help."

"Hop in, Mister Knight-in-shining-armor," D.D. stroked the felt covered steering wheel (the same color as the fat man's fedora). "You can buy me breakfast, a milkshake is about all I can handle, and I'll fill you in."

A short while later we sat across from each other in my usual booth at the Golden Dove. Like D.D.'s battered face, the morning sun brought out the worst in the greasy dive. The waitress set down D.D's strawberry milkshake and slid a plate over to me: piled high with corned beef hash and, of course, a side of bacon. "Thanks, Katya," I said. She refilled my steaming mug and disappeared.

I regaled D.D. with the blow-by-blow of my visit to the Emergency Room: "... and the tetanus shot wasn't too bad. But the rabies shot was a bitch. And Jim tells me I'm going to need another three. After all, who can say where your friend Alex's mouth has been?"

"I know," D.D. nodded. "Alexei Fyodorovich can seem a little unhinged."

"A little?" I said.

"But I guess you'd have to be, you know, a little out there, to believe the off-the-wall stuff he believes." She sipped her milkshake. "I mean, a kind of demon called a Preta managing a bar and grill in Rutherford."

She waited a beat, expecting me to laugh it off.

I didn't.

She continued, "You saw that old book he had, right?"

"I saw a drawing of the tattoo." My voice drifted somewhere faraway. "It's the same one Addie has."

"That's just the tip of the iceberg. Mom's always been a little weird—"

"A little?" I said.

"But I always thought it was mad scientist stuff. And kind of dope. But a few years ago, she really went off the deep end. But that book explains it all. And Alexei Fyodorovich is in with a bunch of guys who, I don't know, battle these demons, or some shit like that." She sucked the straw. There were slurping noises. I ordered her another milkshake. "So, these Pretas, well they, I don't know, their spirits can go hunting, like ghosts that float on bad smells."

"That explains Rutherford," I said. "Right next to the Meadowlands."

"Yeah, Jersey, right? Where else can you find swamps like that? Yeah, so this Preta, his spirit floats on the swamp gas, or whatever, and he can, you know, possess someone. Hijack their minds. Not everyone. Just some people. And then he stamps his brand on them."

"Wow!" I said. "The Preta made Addie do it. I knew it. That's why she made those awful drugs." I slammed my fist on the table. "I just knew it. Well, the good news is, according to Jim, there don't seem to be any more kids with Lazarus Dot overdoses. Just last week, they were pouring into the ER. And now—"

"Yeah," D.D. scoffed. "The supply dried up."

"Wait. What? How do you know—"

"You said you wanted to find my mother," D.D. interrupted. "Why is that? It's not some crazy jilted ex-lover stalkery thing, is it?"

I blushed. "Does she get a lot of that?"

"You have no idea."

"The only reason I'm looking for Addie," I lied, "is to put a stop to the drugs." By the way D.D. eyed me, I knew I was lying badly. "She said she wasn't going to do that kind of stuff anymore." I added wistfully, "She said she was moving to the west coast."

"Sure. The drugs. The infernal drugs," she said. "And all those poor young, hopelessly addicted souls wasting away." She rolled her eye. "Or, even worse, swept away by the grim reaper forever and ever. Into the fathomless abyss."

I dropped my fork. How could someone so young have a voice dripping with so much cynicism?

"So, now the drugs have stopped flowing." D.D. sipped her milkshake. "You've got no more reason to find Mom. Right?" The one eye, which wasn't swollen shut, twinkled mischievously. "You can just get on with your life."

"Yeah, just get on with my life." I folded a strip of bacon into my mouth and chewed pensively. "Yeah, just forget about Addie." I shoveled in the final forkful of hash. "I mean, with the drugs gone." I gulped lukewarm coffee. "On the other hand, if she's tangled up with some Preta, she might be up to her neck in shit."

"Mister Knight-in-shining-armor."

"Doctor Knight-in-shining-armor," I corrected.

"Either way, you may be just what I've been looking for. Just what Mom needs. Alexei Fyodorovich's book explained how to block Preta from controlling Mom's mind."

"I'm all ears."

"Mom's wearing a silver necklace. As long as it's touching her skin, Preta can control her. What I need you to do is grab it."

"Grab Addie's necklace?"

"It'll be a piece of cake. Just yank it off her neck. It's a thin little nothing."

"You want me to steal your mother's necklace?" Something swirled in my brain. I remembered the silver necklace (as delicate as gossamer) and the way it twinkled against her buttery skin. When I'd first met Addie in Prague, she'd told me about some voice in her head. Yeah. That's right. The only way to silence the voice was the necklace. "Wait a minute," I said to D.D.. "Didn't you make that necklace with your own hands? Wasn't wearing the necklace for—"

"You asked who slapped me around," She interrupted. Her voice was colder than her milkshake. "I didn't know for sure until Alexei Fyodorovich read from the book. He told me that the guy who did this," she gestured at her bruised and battered face, "was one of Preta's minions. 'Doing his bidding,' he said, or some shit like that. Preta's not letting Mom go without a fight. He won't let me anywhere within a hundred yards of her. But Preta's flunkies don't have a clue who you are. You can get close to her and… Look, if you're scared, I get it."

I wasn't smart enough to be scared.

Her grin said she knew she had me. She dabbed the blood, which ran from her lip to her chin. "I know where Mom's going to be on Saturday night."

I would highly recommend Rick's, despite what happened between me and Addie that night. It's not for everyone, though. First of all, it's not an easy place to find. It's buried on a backstreet in Secaucus. If you take a left instead of a right off Route 3, you'll be driving in circles for hours, and GPS (with all those route recalculations) just seems to make matters worse. Another thing: Rick's doesn't take credit. They don't take cash either. Only bullion: gold or silver. You've got to leave a deposit with the cashier (who's sequestered behind bullet proof glass) before the *maître d'* will seat you. The minimum is pretty steep: Half an ounce of gold or three pounds of silver.

36

While the cashier weighed out my deposit, I scoped out the place. Black-lacquered paneling and soft light pouring from Tiffany fixtures gave the room an intimate feel, despite its large size. The *maître d'*, who had a Clark-Gable-mustache and slicked back hair, eyed me hungrily. I slipped him a one-ounce silver ingot (which mollified his appetite) and he led me to a good table, near the stage. I settled into a high-backed clamshell seat. The blue velvet wrapped me in privacy and was as soft as a mistress's kiss.

A waiter appeared before my table; a white napkin draped over his sleeve. His tuxedo put the one I wore at my wedding to shame and I'd bet dollars to donuts his bow tie wasn't a clip on. He bowed his head in the quintessential combination of deference and contempt. "What may I bring the gentleman to drink?"

"In a place like this, you've got no choice but martini."

"Very good, sir."

"Hendricks."

"Of course."

"You own the place?" I asked.

"Sir?" He raised his eyebrows.

I gestured towards his name tag.

"Oh." His smirk told me I was the only one not privy to the inside joke. "You'll find we're all named Rick here."

After the third sip of the cocktail (icy shards still somehow swirling around in the gin) the buzz took hold of my brain. It was a mellow buzz. You know the kind. The sounds of the expansive room (clinking silverware, animated conversation and tinkling laughter) expanded and contracted like an accordion.

I ordered the Osso Bucco. The price was listed in the menu .03/3. In other words, the Osso Bucco would set me back either .03 ounces of gold or 3 ounces of silver. It was worth every gram. The meat melted on my tongue and the flavors exploded on my palate like the colors of springtime.

The performances began when the clock struck midnight. Swaying like a willow, under a blue spotlight, I could swear the first guy who climbed onto the stage was George Michael, you know, the guy from Wham. But he's dead. So, it couldn't be him. Anyway, this crooner poured his heart into the microphone. Not-George-Michael wasn't singing one of Wham's early cotton candy songs either. He was belting out *One More Try*. You'd recognize it if it came on the radio: a sad song about star crossed lovers just trying to find some peace.

Rick appeared. The waiter, I mean, not the owner. Another martini (priced at .01/1) precariously balanced upon his tray. I'm no lightweight, but each cocktail packed a wallop like a mule's kick. "I need a breath of air," I gasped.

"Very good, sir." Rick smirked scornfully and pulled back the table without spilling a drop of Hendricks.

I stumbled past the bar on my search for the exit. On another stage (much smaller than the one in the dining room) a veritable Goliath blew sax beneath a blue spotlight. I could swear it was Clarence Clemens, you know, the guy who played in Bruce Springsteen's E Street Band. But, of course, it couldn't be him. He's dead.

Not-Clarence launched into his uber-funky take on Herb Alpert's *Rise*. His eyes were glued to a curvy figure who leaned against the bar. She was striking; tall for a woman, with long braids hanging down her broad back. That hair reminded me of Holly, my favorite bartender. But it couldn't be her. Holly's hair was golden and silky. This lady's hair was coarse and faded, like autumn hay.

Still, I crept a little closer. Those couldn't be Holly's hands. They were the liver-spotted, veiny hands of a much older woman and the knuckles were gnarled by arthritis. I leaned against the bar to get a gander at her profile. The skin sagged from her high cheekbones and there were deep wrinkles around her—

She must have felt the weight of my stare. She turned towards me.

The sadness in her sky-blue eyes blanketed me like a mist and made it more than a little hard to breathe. "Holly?"

She covered her wrinkled face with her arthritic hands. "What are *you* doing here?"

"Is it really you?" I asked. "What happened to you?" I was smart enough not to add, 'you look forty years older than the last time I saw you.' "And what happened to Azazel's?"

"I never wanted you to see me like this," she said and fled.

I chased her into the street but she was gone, as if she'd evaporated into a beam of moonlight. "Curiouser and curiouser," I said.

By the time I returned to my table, Not-George-Michael was gone and a baby grand piano had appeared on the stage. The pianist stepped from behind the blue velvet curtain. Applause accompanied her to the bench. She nodded haughtily. They'd all been waiting for her and she knew it. A spaghetti strap, full-length gown hugged her lithe body like a second skin.

Music filled the air. Oh, the way she shut her eyes (so tight) and tossed her head backwards. Addie was one with the instrument; her fingers bled into the depthless ebony keys. How I wish those nimble digits were brushing my quivering flesh instead. Oh, the way her lips curled and danced with the music. A dusky hue settled upon her soft cheeks. Watching the pink blotches blossom on her elegant neck and the blue veins engorge, I felt in my guts exactly what kind of music we would make between the sheets. I'd have walked over burning coals to tickle those ivories.

The notes lingered in the air after she finished the piece. I'll never be able to hear Liszt again without my heart skipping a beat. But even the most magical moment can't last forever. The music faded.

I leapt onto the stage and the audience gasped.

Addie swiveled on the lacquered bench and gazed up at me. Her David-Bowie-eyes (each a gem of a different color) glittered under the spotlight. "Oh, Felix," she said. Her haughtiness melted. She looked at me as if I were a knight in shining armor. "I knew you'd come for me."

My cheeks blazed. My mouth fell open. The words filling my heart got stuck somewhere. All I could say was, "Addie, I…"

Her gaze fell upon my fist.

I unfurled my fingers. Draped across my palm (the silver like gossamer) was the chain D.D. had crafted (link by link) with her own hands.

Addie's eyes widened in terror.

An odor (like puked up rotten eggs) suddenly suffused the restaurant. Several in the audience groaned. It was as if the awful stench were crouching at the door, waiting for its moment to leap in and submerge us all.

The fear in Addie's eyes was gone now and they glistened with sadness and her face grew infinitely weary. "Oh, Felix," she repeated. "I don't know who's the bigger fool. Me, for earnestly making a promise, which in my heart I knew I couldn't keep. Or you, for believing it."

"Addie, I…"

The muscles of her face quivered as if invisible tiny horsemen were galloping across its hills and valleys. When the motion stopped, she looked different, yet the same. She'd become the most profane version of herself. "I never wanted you to see me like this, Felix," she said and turned away.

The tattoo at the intersection of her neck, back and shoulder grew blacker and blacker until it vacuumed up all the light around it. The symbols comprising the three intertwined rings grew crisper and sharper and ever more hypnotic. The tattoo called to me, but not all of me, just the worst parts. All shadow, no light. It would be so easy: Drifting away like a puff of smoke. So very easy.

Addie turned her face towards me. A wicked smile curled her lip and her eyes were icy. "You can join us, you know."

The depraved tone in her voice was a bucket of cold water dumped over my head. "I can, Addie. But I won't." I've never been one to choose the easy path. "And you don't need to… to… to go there, either."

Addie popped up from the piano bench and flew into my arms. Her embrace grew tighter and tighter, like a python coiled around my spine. She reached under my shirt and raked her nails down my back. The audience 'oohed' and 'ahhed,' as if it were all part of the show. She reached into my trousers and worked her way around, back to front.

"Hey, we're in public, here," I said. Laughter filled the room, like the soundtrack in a '70s sit-com.

She found what she was looking for. The audience gasped. My mouth dropped open too. Addie was aiming Alex Whatever-ovich's pearl handled Colt at my chest.

"Felix," she implored, "tell me true: Do you love me?"

I wanted to lie. I really did. And not simply because I was staring down the barrel of a gun. I almost loved her.

Someone in the audience shouted, "Say it!"

And it wasn't such a far stretch, either. But the prohibition against bearing false witness was the only commandment I'd left unbroken. If I violated that one…

"It's alright, Felix," she said. "It's for the better, really. Even if you gave me your heart. I wouldn't have been satisfied until I owned your soul." She flipped the revolver around and stuck the business end into her mouth. Mocha lipstick wrapped around cold steel. She pulled the trigger and splattered the black-lacquered piano with her brains.

Chapter Six
Facing the Music

When I finally worked up the nerve to face D.D., enough time had passed for her black eye to fade and busted lip to heal. She looked like a fresh-faced debutante. My visage, on the other hand, was ashen and drawn. I stepped shakily into her kitchen and squinted into the harsh fluorescent glare. She glanced over at me and said, "You look like a pile of shit."

My grumbling stomach and the ticking clock on the wall told me it was dinner time. She was frying up a big fat pancake in a cast iron skillet. The pale surface bubbled and she flipped it. The underside was crisp and golden brown. My mouth watered. She asked, "You want plain or chocolate chip?"

"If it's not too much trouble," I said. "Maybe you could make mine blueberry."

She grumbled about overly demanding guests who weren't even invited and tugged the refrigerator door. I expected to see the gateway to a secret dimension. She rifled through the shelves (disappointingly mundane) and pulled out a carton of blueberries. Maybe I'd just imagined her and Alex Whatevero-vich jumping into the refrigerator and disappearing from this world. I've certainly had stranger dreams.

She tossed a handful of berries into the batter. The sound of sizzling soon filled the air. It smelled like heaven on earth.

"Take a seat," she ordered. She set plates and butter and maple syrup down onto the Formica table. I devoured ambrosia by the forkful. Fluffy as clouds. She smirked at my rapturous expression with the haughtiness of one to whom displays of emotion are merely betrayals of weakness. "Eat much?"

"You might say, I've been on an all-liquid diet," I said. "For days and days."

"Another?" She asked.

I nodded, like Oliver Twist in the orphanage scene. You know the one.

"You've got something for me?" She demanded.

I wasn't hungry anymore. I felt the moment of truth rushing towards me like a freight train. I'd been hoping to scarf down another pancake or two before D.D. started the inquisition. I fished the fine silver chain from my pocket and slid it across the table.

Her smile turned toothy. "Well, well, well, Mister Knight-in-shining-armor completed his quest after all." She pocketed the silver and sauntered to the stove, which was behind me.

I gazed at my plate: the sticky puddle of maple syrup: the sodden pancake crumbs.

D.D spoke as she mixed up another bowlful of batter. "Tell me about your little adventure at Rick's. I've heard that place is totally out of this world. I wish I could've been there. I'd love to have heard Mom play. In another life she could've been Khatia Buniatishvili." She ladled the mix onto the skillet and it began to sizzle. "It's been ages. But Jersey… you know."

The first pancake (so delicious when it slid down my throat) turned to a lump of clay in my gullet.

"I would kill to have seen the look on Mom's face when you yanked off the chain." She laughed, hollow and jaded. "How did our damsel in distress—"

"D.D.," I interrupted. "She… Well, I don't know how to say this… She's dead." I moaned. "Addie's dead."

"What?"

"Your mom… well, she… she killed herself."

"You worthless sack of shit," she hissed.

"I'm so sorry, D.D.," I said. "I really am." I buried my face in my hands. "I tried to stop her." I moaned. "I really did. But she just grabbed my gun and—"

"Who's going to replenish my stash now?"

"What? Stash?" My innards turned to ice. "What are you talking about?"

"The other chemists can't make heads or tails of those damned recipes without her."

"Recipes?" I turned and cocked my head. "What?" I gulped but my throat was dry. "You can't possibly mean the designer drugs? The Lazarus Dot? I mean, it killed all those kids."

She dumped the pancake into the trash.

"Hey," I said. "I was going to eat that."

"On to plan B, I guess." D.D. said and smashed the frying pan across my face.

Made in the USA
Middletown, DE
02 November 2023

41821187R00027